The Pixie Mix-Up

~❧ Book One ❧~

DISNEY PRESS
New York

Illustrated by the Disney Storybook Artists
Designed by Deborah Boone

Printed in China

First Edition
1 3 5 7 9 10 8 6 4 2

Library of Congress Catalog Card Number on file.

ISBN 978-1-4231-2590-7
F904-9088-1-10135

For more Disney Press fun,
visit www.disneybooks.com

One morning, just after dawn, Tinker Bell was hard at work putting a new weather vane on a high branch of the Home Tree.

She had just tapped the last nail into place when a gust of wind swept past the tree. It was so strong it lifted Tink right off the branch.

She watched the weather vane spin. *Could it be?* Tink wondered. She sniffed the air. It smelled clean and fresh.

"It's the Spring Breeze!" Tink cried. "Time for spring-cleaning!"

The Spring Breeze swept through the Home Tree, waking the other fairies. Soon, the polishing-talent fairies were busy buffing the walls and windows till they sparkled. The keyhole-design fairies cleaned all the locks, and the décor-talent fairies aired out the curtains. For whenever the Spring Breeze arrived in Pixie Hollow, the fairies knew it was time to set things right in the Home Tree.

Tink was on her way to tidy up her workshop when she heard someone call her name.

"Tink! Down here!" The garden fairy Lily waved to her from the roots of the Home Tree. "I'm planting new flowers," Lily told Tink. "But I need to get my spare trowel. Would you mind watering the flowers while I'm gone? I'll only be a moment."

"Sure," Tink said. "Go right ahead."

Lifting Lily's watering can, Tink sprinkled water on the first flower. Drip, drip, drip. The water trickled slowly from the can.

Tink sighed with frustration. *It will take all day to water these flowers!* she thought. *Isn't there some way to make the job go faster?* Suddenly Tink had an idea.

Within moments, the crafty tinker fairy had built a supersize sprinkler! As she pulled a long vine, a row of watering cans tilted, gently showering the flowers with water.

Tink smiled. This job would be done in no time, and then she could get to her workshop to finish up her tinker tasks.

Meanwhile, Lily was hurrying through the courtyard, on her way to her room, when Rani stopped her.

"Oh, Lily!" Rani said. "Could you do me a favor?"

"Of course," said Lily.

Rani pointed to a stream of soapy water that was swirling all around. "I'm washing the courtyard, but I've run out of soap. Could you keep an eye on things here while I go get more?"

Lily nodded. *What could be simpler?,* she thought.

One minute passed, then two, then three. Lily was eager to get back to her flowers. If only she could speed things up!

In her garden, Lily helped flowers grow by sprinkling them with fairy dust and whispering words of encouragement.

"Come on, bubbles. Get bigger! You can do it." she whispered, throwing fairy dust on them.

The bubbles began to grow. With soap bubbles this big, the courtyard would be clean in a snap!

Inside the Home Tree, Rani hurried down the hall. As she passed the tearoom, she heard a strange sound. *Chee-cheee!*

Rani looked inside. The animal-talent fairy Beck was dusting the tearoom with the help of some squirrels.

"Chee-cheee," Beck said in Squirrel. *"Cheee-rup!"*

"Oh, Rani!" Beck said, spotting her friend. "I'm so glad to see you. I need to find some nuts for my friends here. Could you point out the dusty spots to them, while I fly off for a second?"

Rani said she'd be glad to help.

Rani watched the squirrels. She pointed out the spots that needed dusting. But the squirrels weren't paying attention.

Rani frowned. At this rate, the dusting would never get done! She wished she could speak Squirrel. *"Cheee-cheee!"* Rani said, trying to imitate Beck.

The squirrels froze.

They understood me! Rani thought. *"Cheee, cheee!"* she said again.

The squirrels panicked. They ran through the tearoom, knocking over tables and chairs.

Beck quickly flew back into the room. "What's going on?" she cried.

"I just told them to dust over there," said Rani. "Like this: *'Cheee, cheee!'*"

"That doesn't mean 'Dust over there,'" shouted Beck. "That means, 'Look out for that hawk!'"

The squirrels raced out of the tearoom, with Beck and Rani on their heels.

"What's this?" Rani cried when they reached the door. The courtyard was filled with gigantic bubbles!

The squirrels couldn't stop. They skidded across the soapy courtyard and flew through the air.

"Look out!" yelled Tink.

But it was too late. The squirrels crashed into Tink's watering-can sprinkler. Water splashed everywhere.

Tink, Lily, Rani, and Beck looked around the courtyard. It was full of soggy laundry, soapy flowers, and unhappy fairies.

"I'd fly backward if I could," Rani told Beck. "I didn't mean to scare the squirrels."

"I'd fly backward if I could," Lily told Rani. "I guess I made the bubbles a little too big."

"I'd fly backward if I could," Tink told Lily. "Maybe I used too much water."

"Look at this mess!" a laundry-talent fairy exclaimed angrily. "It's worse than when we started. You'd all better get to work cleaning."

And that's exactly what they did.
When they were finished, the Home Tree
had never looked better.